YOU CHOOSE
BOOKS

Sleeping Beauty

AN INTERACTIVE FAIRY TALE ADVENTURE

by Jessica Gunderson

illustrated by
Mariano Epelbaum

Raintree is an imprint of Capstone Global Library Limited, a company incorporated in England and Wales having its registered office at 264 Banbury Road, Oxford, OX2 7DY – Registered company number: 6695582

www.raintree.co.uk
myorders@raintree.co.uk

Edited by Michelle Hasselius
Designed by Heidi Thompson
Original illustrations © Capstone Global Library Limited 2019
Picture research by Jo Miller
Production by Tori Abraham
Originated by Capstone Global Library Ltd
Printed and bound in India

ISBN 978 1 4747 6341 7
22 21 20 19 18
10 9 8 7 6 5 4 3 2 1

British Library Cataloguing in Publication Data
A full catalogue record for this book is available from the British Library.

Acknowledgements
We would like to thank the following for permission to reproduce images:
Shutterstock: solarbird, background

Contents

About your adventure

You live a life that most people can only dream of. But that dream is about to turn into a nightmare. Open your eyes before it's too late!

In this fairy tale, you control your fate. Wake up and make your choices to determine what happens next.

Chapter One sets the scene. Then you choose which path to read. Follow the directions at the bottom of the page as you read the stories. The decisions you make will change your outcome. After you've finished one path, go back and read the others for new perspectives and more adventures.

Beauty sleep

Sleep is a wonderful thing – quiet and peaceful. But not when it's forever.

You must be careful. Somewhere a sharp needle glistens, waiting for blood. Who will be next – your friends? Your family? Perhaps the needle is waiting for you. You could be doomed to a lifetime of eternal slumber.

You must make the right choices. Find a way to wake those up around you and bring them out of the darkness.

TO BE ROSE, A PRINCESS TRAPPED IN HER CASTLE ON HER BIRTHDAY, TURN TO PAGE 9.

TO BE MILLICENT, WHO JUST WANTS TO GO TO A PARTY, TURN TO PAGE 45.

TO BE BRIAR, A SPACE WARRIOR FIGHTING THE EVIL FAIRY AND HER ALIEN MINIONS, TURN TO PAGE 79.

CHAPTER 2

The birthday party

You've lived your whole life locked away in a castle. It's a big castle, but the walls have always felt like they're closing in on you. You could say that your parents – the king and queen of the realm – are overprotective. You are forbidden from touching anything sharp. They act like it'll *kill* you or something. Talk about dramatic! Your father has even ordered that all spinning wheels in the kingdom be burned.

You're not allowed to set foot outside. Inside the castle the servants follow you around like trained dogs. The only place you're ever alone is in your bedroom. You spend your days reading books about adventures in faraway places.

It's been like this for as long as you can remember. And you're nearly sixteen years old! Your parents won't tell you why they are so worried, but you've heard whispers from the servants. According to them, your parents had a grand party when you were born. They invited everyone in the kingdom – everyone except for an evil fairy called Raven. But Raven came anyway. She stood over your cot and swore that one day, you would prick your finger and die. Then she disappeared into a cloud of purple smoke. As soon as she had gone, another fairy stepped forward and waved a wand. The fairy assured your parents that you wouldn't die – only sleep.

The whole thing sounds ridiculous to you. No one dies from pricking their finger! As your sixteenth birthday approaches, you decide to take a stand. You go to your parents as they lounge by the fire.

"Mum and Dad," you say confidently. "I know what I want for my birthday."

"What is that, Rose?" asks your mother, looking up from her knitting.

"I want to have a party," you say. "And I want to invite the whole kingdom!"

"Absolutely not!" says your father crossly. "It's much too dangerous."

"I could do with a little danger in my life," you say through hot tears. "You keep me locked in this castle like a prisoner!"

"That's enough, Rose," says your father sternly. "If you continue to act this way, you can go to your room."

TO KEEP BEGGING FOR A PARTY, TURN TO PAGE 12.

TO GO TO YOUR ROOM, TURN TO PAGE 27.

You beg and beg for a party, but your father won't give in. You run upstairs to your room and slam the door so hard that the whole castle shakes. You throw yourself on your bed and cry yourself to sleep. When you wake up an hour later, you can hear your parents talking in the corridor. You get up and put your ear to the door so you can hear what they're saying.

"I know you don't want a party, but Rose is getting older," your mother says. "We should start letting her do some things, or she'll rebel. We don't want her running off with that Robin Hood boy."

12

"True," your father agrees. "I've heard that boy is a thief!"

"And if we have a party here, we can keep an eye on her," your mother adds.

"We'll employ every armed guard in the kingdom," your father says.

Soon you hear a soft knock at your door. Your parents come in, beaming as though they are parents of the year.

"You may have a birthday party at the castle," your father tells you. You wrap your arms around your parents and thank them happily.

The morning of your birthday, all of the servants are busy preparing for the party. It's been a long time since visitors have been allowed inside the castle. Cooks rush around the kitchen, preparing a feast. Maids clean and dust every bit of the castle until it sparkles.

TURN THE PAGE.

You step out of your room and look around. The corridor is completely empty. You can't believe it. Everyone is so busy getting ready for the party, no one has time to watch you!

You've never truly been on your own in the castle. You wander around until you notice a door at the end of a long corridor. The door is always locked, but today it is open just a crack. You are about to go inside when you hear voices along the corridor behind you.

"Rose, Rose, the belle of the ball," a female voice sings.

"We will make her prettier than all!" shrills another voice.

"But there's still something left to do," says a third voice. "Just another stitch or two."

You are startled, but curious. What are they singing about? Perhaps they have a gift for your birthday! On the other hand, you have no idea who these women are. Your father has always warned you to stay away from strangers. What if they mean you harm?

TO TALK TO THE WOMEN, TURN TO PAGE 16.

TO AVOID THE WOMEN AND OPEN THE DOOR, TURN TO PAGE 19.

You refuse to let fear rule your life. Besides, these women look like they wouldn't harm a fly.

"Hello," you say, approaching the three women. "My name is Rose. Are you singing about me?"

The women look at each other and giggle. "Yes, of course!" says one of them. She is dressed in a green dress with a matching green cape and hat. "And we have a gift for you, Rose. Follow us."

You follow the women to a tiny room that you've never been in before. There is a beautiful pink-and-blue gown on a table in the middle of the room.

"We are fairies, Rose," says the woman in green. "Many years ago, we protected you from an evil fairy's curse."

"What do you mean, *we?*" snaps the second woman. She is dressed in yellow. "*I* am the one who reversed the curse."

"Yes, Marigold," says the third woman, rolling her eyes. She is dressed in dark blue. She turns to you. "I'm Iris, and this is Marigold and Poppy. We have been protecting you ever since Raven put a curse on you all those years ago. And now that you are turning sixteen, we must be even more vigilant."

17

You're not really listening to Iris and the other fairies. You keep looking at the gorgeous gown on the table.

"Is this for me?" you ask, pointing to the gown.

TURN THE PAGE.

"Yes," Poppy says. "It's for you to wear to the party tonight. And don't worry, we'll be watching you every second."

"Every second?" you ask with a gulp.

"Yes, absolutely!" says Poppy cheerfully. "We'll be with you the whole night." Marigold and Iris nod. "Now we still have to finish your dress," says Poppy. "Wait in your room. We'll bring it to you."

The fairies are going to be with you the whole night? Your heart sinks. This is exactly what you didn't want. For years you've wondered what it would be like to leave the castle, even for a day. Perhaps you should miss the party and find out. Then again, this is the first party your parents have let you have in sixteen years. How hard would it be to lose a few fairies?

TO GO BACK TO YOUR ROOM, TURN TO PAGE 25.

TO MISS THE PARTY, TURN TO PAGE 27.

You step through the door and enter a small room. In the middle of the room, an old woman sits at a spinning wheel. The fabric she is weaving is beautiful and sparkling gold.

"What are you doing?" you ask. You've never seen a spinning wheel up close before.

"Eh?" says the old woman. "I can't hear you. Come closer."

You walk over to the old woman and speak up. "I said, what are you doing?" you shout.

"I am spinning, my child," the woman says.

"But the king has ordered all spinning wheels in this kingdom to be burned," you tell her.

She looks at you, surprised. "Really?" she says. "I've never heard such an order. I'm hard of hearing, you know."

You watch as she spins the wheel and weaves golden strands.

"Magical," you say under your breath.

"Would you like to try?" the old woman asks.

You hesitate. You know you should tell your father. After all, having a spinning wheel is against the law. But the wheel looks harmless. Perhaps you should try it, just this once.

TO TRY YOUR HAND AT THE SPINNING WHEEL, TURN TO PAGE 21.

TO RUN AWAY AND TELL YOUR FATHER, TURN TO PAGE 22.

"Oh, what fun!" you say. "I would love to try." You take a seat at the spinning wheel.

"Be careful," the woman warns. "The spindle is sharp!" But as soon as the words leave her mouth, you prick your finger on the spindle.

"Ouch!" you yell. Blood appears on your finger. Your head spins. "My head feels fuzzy."

"Why don't you lie down on this soft bed and rest," the woman says.

As you climb onto the bed, you take another look at the old woman. But she's not an old woman any more. Instead, she has transformed into a fairy in a purple-and-black dress. Raven!

21

You sleep for a hundred years. In your dreams, you wait for your prince to come and rescue you.

THE END
TO FOLLOW ANOTHER PATH, TURN TO PAGE 7.

You turn and run out of the room as fast as you can to find your father. He's in the ballroom, overseeing preparations for the party.

"Father! I just met a strange old woman upstairs," you tell him breathlessly. "And she has a spinning wheel!"

His face darkens. "Guards!" he calls. Four large guards rush to the king's side. He turns to you. "Show us where she is, Rose," he says.

You lead the way down the long corridor and push open the door to the room.

22

"You've returned, my dear," the old woman croaks when you enter. "Would you like to try my spinning wheel now?"

The old woman stands up and hobbles towards you. Then she sees the guards. Her face twists into an angry scowl.

Before your eyes, the old woman starts to grow taller. Her grey hair turns to midnight black. Her tattered dress changes into a long purple-and-black gown. You stare at her in horror.

"It's Raven!" cries the king. "Seize her at once!" The guards charge at Raven. But she only laughs.

"This is not over! I will have my revenge," Raven hisses. Then with a wave of her hand, she disappears in a puff of smoke.

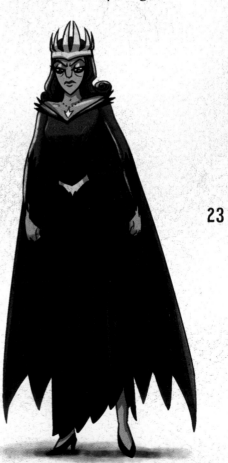

23

"Burn the spinning wheel," your father commands. The guards throw the spinning wheel into the fireplace. It burns to a crisp as strange purple smoke fills the air.

"The party is off," he says. "Close the gate. Guards, take my daughter back to her room and wait outside her door. We can't take any chances."

You are taken back to your bedroom. The heavy door slams shut behind you. You throw yourself on your bed as tears run down your face. Without the party, it doesn't feel like much of a birthday any more. You're trapped in the castle again. And with Raven on the loose, you know this is how you'll spend the rest of your days.

THE END
TO FOLLOW ANOTHER PATH, TURN TO PAGE 7.

You wait and wait in your room, until finally there is a light knock at your door. You open it and a beautiful fairy waltzes in. She's dressed in a dark dress that shimmers as she walks.

"Hello, my child," she says. You look down at the fairy's hands. She isn't carrying your gown.

"Who are you?" you ask.

"Oh, didn't the three fairies tell you about me?" the fairy asks. "I'm one of the other fairies."

You look at her suspiciously. Poppy, Iris and Marigold didn't mention anything about another fairy. Or did they? You start to back away slowly.

"Who are you?" you ask again, dreading the answer. "What is your name?"

"Why, I am Raven, of course," she says, moving towards you. "And I have a story to tell you."

TO HEAR RAVEN'S STORY, TURN TO PAGE 30.

TO THROW HER OUT OF YOUR ROOM, TURN TO PAGE 33.

"Fine," you say with a sigh. "I'll go."

As you walk along the corridor to your bedroom, you look out of the window and see the Enchanted Forest. It's just outside the castle gate. You've never explored it on your own before.

"I'm sick of people following me around," you say to yourself. "For once, I'm going to do what I want to do!"

You go back to your bedroom and get an old cloak from your wardrobe. You put it over your shoulders and pull the hood over your head. Then you slip out of the castle, taking care not to be seen. When you get outside, you run across the courtyard, through the castle gate and into the Enchanted Forest. You keep running until you can't see the castle behind you any more. You let your hood drop and take a deep breath of fresh air. At long last, you are outside!

You follow a path that twists and turns through the trees. As you walk, you listen to the birds singing in the branches above you. You feel the crunch of twigs and leaves under your feet. You've never felt so free!

After a while you see a tall, lone tower rising above the trees. The place looks spooky and mysterious, like something from one of the fairy tales you've read. You'd love to explore it! Suddenly you hear a rustling through the trees. You duck behind a large oak tree and peer down the path.

A handsome young man on a horse is weaving his way through the forest. You recognize him as the prince from the nearby kingdom. He pats the horse's neck.

"The castle must be around here somewhere," the prince says.

He must be on his way to my party, you think.
The party might not be so bad after all.

You could offer to show him the way to
the castle. You could share a first dance in the
ballroom. But going back to the castle means
going back to all the rules and restrictions. This
may be your only chance to explore the tower.

29

TO APPROACH THE PRINCE, TURN TO PAGE 35.

TO EXPLORE THE TOWER, TURN TO PAGE 38.

"What story?" you ask cautiously. "And where are the other fairies?"

"They are fine," Raven says. "They have almost finished with your dress. We have to talk quickly."

Raven moves closer until she is standing at the foot of your bed. "I'm sure the fairies told you about your first party, when you were a baby," she says. "People came from far and wide to see you. Everyone was invited, except me," says Raven with a hint of sadness. She continues. "I was furious. When I made my grand entrance, I wanted to scare your parents. But I didn't *curse* you. I only said I hoped you would prick your finger. Over the years, the story grew. I was made out to be some sort of fire-breathing dragon!"

Raven pauses and lets out a tired sigh.
"I shouldn't have said what I said all those years
ago. But I don't deserve all of this. I've been
banished from the kingdom, forced to look over
my shoulder for years. I wanted you to know the
truth, and this was my first chance to tell you."

Raven covers her face and begins to sob.
You believe her. You touch her shoulder.

"I never believed there was a curse," you tell
her. She doesn't stop crying. "It looks like we are
both victims of someone else's fear. I'm sorry you
were treated this way for so long."

Raven hiccups, tears streaming down her face.
You have an idea. You tell Raven to wait in your
bedroom. Moments later, you come back with
your parents. They listen to Raven's story and
reluctantly apologize to her.

You turn to Raven. "You weren't invited to my first party, but you are to this one. Raven, will you come to my birthday party?" you ask.

"Oh yes, I would love to!" Raven exclaims.

The night of your party, you dance the night away with a prince from another kingdom. As you spin around the ballroom, you look back. All the fairies are happily watching you dance, including Raven.

THE END
TO FOLLOW ANOTHER PATH, TURN TO PAGE 7.

"Leave my room at once, you evil witch!" you yell, shaking in fear. "Help! Someone help!"

"How dare you!" Raven snarls, as her pleasant expression turns fierce. She steps towards you. You cower behind your bed. You look around. You have nothing to protect yourself with.

"Precious, protected princess," Raven hisses. "You deserve every word of my curse!"

Raven lunges at you, and you make a run for your bedroom door. You're almost there, when she whirls in front of you – a mass of black and purple smoke. Then she transforms into a giant spinning wheel!

You try to move away but are pulled towards the spindle. Your hand raises unwillingly, and the spindle pricks your index finger. A small trail of blood drips down your hand.

Instantly, you slump to the floor. Your entire body is paralysed. Raven lets out an evil laugh and transforms back into herself again.

As your eyes close, she leans over you. "Sleep well, my pretty," she cackles.

THE END
TO FOLLOW ANOTHER PATH, TURN TO PAGE 7.

"Hello, there," you say, stepping out onto the path. "My name is Princess Rose. You must be on your way to my party."

The prince stares at you, surprised. "Hello, Princess," he says, bowing his head. "May I ask what you are doing out in the woods all alone?"

You think quickly. "I was gathering berries for my party," you say. "But I couldn't find any. Will you escort me back to the castle?"

He smiles. "I would be delighted."

When you get back to the castle, you put on the dress that the fairies have made for you. It's perfect. It shimmers in blue and pink. You glide into the party on the prince's arm. Everyone stares in awe. He leads you to the dance floor as the music starts to play.

Just as you are about to begin the first dance, you hear a loud crash. The castle door flies open and in walks a tall, beautiful fairy.

"Raven!" gasps one of the guests.

"I hear there's a party," Raven says as she walks to the centre of the room. "My, my. It looks like my invitation was lost in the post again. No matter, I've come to finish what I started all those years ago." She lifts her magical staff and points it straight at you. The prince steps in front of you and draws his sword.

"Not this time, Raven!" cries Iris. The three fairies jump in front of the prince and point their wands at Raven. Streaks of blue, pink and green hit Raven with a thud. Raven points her staff, but she is no match for the fairies' combined powers. They hit Raven again. This time, she is turned into a puff of smoke.

She'll never bother you again," Marigold says. The crowd cheers. The music starts up again, and you and the prince dance all night.

Now that Raven is no longer a threat, your parents let you do all the things normal princesses do. You go riding in the Enchanted Forest. You attend royal balls. And eventually you marry the prince. You both live happily ever after.

THE END

TO FOLLOW ANOTHER PATH, TURN TO PAGE 7.

You can't lose the chance to explore the tower. You wait for the prince to pass by on his horse and make your way to the tower. It is even darker and gloomier up close. It looks like it's been abandoned for years.

You pull down the vines that cover the door. The door handle looks rusted, but luckily it's easy to turn. Inside the tower, you see a sweeping staircase. You tiptoe up the stairs, your footsteps echoing in the silence. You shiver, but you keep going. At the top of the stairs, you find yourself in a dark, shadowy room. As your eyes adjust to the darkness, you see something move in the corner. You freeze. The tower isn't abandoned after all.

"So we meet again," says a raspy voice.
A match strikes. The eerie glow of a lantern
illuminates a woman in a long, dark gown.

You know instantly that it's Raven. She
cackles and touches a spinning wheel at her side.

"Come closer, my dear," Raven says.

A great magical force draws you towards
Raven and the spinning wheel. You try to run,
but something keeps pulling you closer to
the wheel.

TO FALL UNDER RAVEN'S SPELL, TURN TO PAGE 40.

TO FIGHT AGAINST RAVEN'S POWER, TURN TO PAGE 42.

"No!" you cry loudly. "I won't give in to you!" You resist the magical force with all your might.

As you struggle, you can hear Raven's evil cackling. The spinning wheel keeps drawing your body closer, like a magnet. Your finger touches the spindle.

"No!" you cry. The last thing you hear is Raven's voice.

"Sweet dreams . . . for a century!" she laughs.

You fall into a deep, dark sleep. Time passes, but you continue to sleep. Thorny rose vines cover the tower and the rest of the castle grounds. The castle falls into ruins. The sky is always dark, and the birds stop singing.

Then one day years later, you are woken from your slumber. You open your eyes and let out a big yawn.

A young man stands by your bedside. He has thorny vines stuck in his hair.

"Princess Rose, you are awake!" he exclaims.

"Hello," you say. "Thank you for saving me." You have a feeling you will be seeing a lot more of him in the years to come.

THE END
TO FOLLOW ANOTHER PATH, TURN TO PAGE 7.

You float towards Raven. Her eyes glow green in the light of the lantern.

"Just give the wheel a little spin," Raven urges.

Your hand unwillingly moves towards the spinning wheel. As you are pulled closer, you raise your other arm with all your might. You knock over the lantern, which crashes to the floor. The wooden spinning wheel erupts into flames.

"No!" cries Raven, as the fire starts to spread. "What have you done, you foolish girl?"

The magic pulling you is broken. You turn and run from the room. As you bolt down the steps, you can hear Raven screaming.

"I'll get you!" Raven yells.

You don't stop running until you reach your father in the castle. You lead him and his guards through the Enchanted Forest.

When you come to where the tower stood, it is destroyed. All that's left of the tower – and Raven – is a pile of ashes.

Your father looks at you. "Is that . . . ?" he asks.

"Yes, that's Raven," you say. You turn to face your father. "I'm sorry that I didn't listen," you sigh. "If I had just stayed in the castle, none of this would have happened."

Your father smiles. "No, Rose," he says. "I underestimated you. I should have known you were strong enough to defeat Raven."

You and your father share a hug and turn towards the castle. "It looks like you've missed your own party," says your father. "But come, I have someone I'd like you to meet. He is a prince from the nearby kingdom."

43

THE END
TO FOLLOW ANOTHER PATH, TURN TO PAGE 7.

CHAPTER 3

The uninvited guest

You are one of the richest people in Castle City, but no amount of money can make you happy. You used to be a social butterfly, invited to every party in town. But not any more.

It could be because of all the accidents you keep having. At Cinderella's birthday party, you tripped and knocked over the punch bowl. It spilled bright-red punch all over the birthday girl's dress. But really, she shouldn't have been standing so close to red punch. At another party, you left the front door open. The hosts' prize-winning dalmatians escaped. But they found the dogs – all 101 of them.

It all started about sixteen years ago.
Since then, you haven't had one bit of luck.
You attended a party celebrating the birth of
Rachel King. You didn't receive an invitation, but
that was obviously a mistake. After all, everyone
else was invited. You decided to just sneak inside
and blend in with the crowd.

The proud Kings passed their new baby girl
around. When it was your turn to hold her,
you cradled Rachel gently. Then you noticed one
of the gifts for the baby behind you. It was an
antique, gold-plated spinning wheel.

"Who gives a baby a spinning wheel?" you
asked. "She could prick her finger and die!"

Suddenly the chattering crowd fell silent.
Everyone stared at you in shock.

"What did she say?" asked a guest.

"She threatened the baby!" cried another.

"No, no, that's not what I meant," you tried to explain. But it was too late.

"Get out of here, Millicent Fairy!" Mr King thundered at you. "You weren't even invited to this party!" After that, you never received another invitation in Castle City.

Then one day you are browsing the society pages online. A headline pops up on your screen: YOUNG SOCIALITE RACHEL KING TO CELEBRATE HER SIXTEENTH BIRTHDAY TONIGHT AT THE BLACK TOWER HOTEL.

This could be my chance to make things right, you think.

You could go to the party, explain that everything was a big misunderstanding, and give Rachel a gift. It's perfect! There's only one problem – you aren't invited.

That's never stopped me before, you think.

You rush to the shops and buy Rachel a golden fidget spinner in the shape of a spinning wheel – a little joke about the last time you met. Now how do you get it to her? You could sneak in, like you did last time. Or you could linger outside the hotel and wait for Rachel to arrive. Then you could explain everything to her.

48

TO SNEAK INTO THE BIRTHDAY PARTY, TURN TO PAGE 49.

TO WAIT OUTSIDE FOR RACHEL, TURN TO PAGE 50.

You decide to make an appearance at the party. After all, it's been years. What are the chances anyone will recognize you? You look through your wardrobe and find a black dress. Everyone wears black these days. You'll easily blend in.

On the night of the party, your limo pulls up at the hotel. Guests are filing in through the front doors. The bouncer at the entrance is checking invitations. You don't think you can slip past him, so you sneak around the back.

Luckily the back door is open. The caterer has propped it open to deliver the trays of food. When you get inside, you notice Rachel hasn't made her entrance yet.

49

TO JOIN THE GUESTS IN THE BALLROOM, TURN TO PAGE 52.

TO LOOK FOR RACHEL, TURN TO PAGE 68.

You set off for the Black Tower Hotel. You tell your limo driver to stop a street away and walk the rest of the way.

The hotel is lit up. Lights glow out of every window. As you approach, you hear the sweet sounds of music and laughter. You take a deep breath and enjoy the moment. Oh, how you've missed this!

Just then a group of party guests walks towards you, carrying gifts. You get nervous and dive behind the bushes near the hotel. As you wait for them to pass, you touch the spinning wheel fidget spinner in your pocket. You can't wait to give it to Rachel.

"Hello there! Are you here for Rachel's party?" a male voice says behind you. You jump, startled. You turn to see a handsome young man wearing a suit and a pink tie, peering down at your hiding place.

"I . . . um . . . ," you stammer.

"I'm Phil," he says, extending his hand. "Let me escort you in."

What luck! This could be your chance to get inside the party. Walking in with an invited guest is almost like you were invited too. But what if someone recognizes you? You might be better off waiting here for Rachel.

TO GO INSIDE WITH PHIL, TURN TO PAGE 54.

TO STAY OUTSIDE, TURN TO PAGE 56.

You step into the ballroom, and everybody turns to stare at you. You look around the room and see that absolutely everyone is wearing pink. Except you. You thought you'd blend in by wearing black. Instead, you stand out like a sore thumb. Your embarrassed face turns as pink as all of those dresses.

You hear guests starting to whisper. "Didn't she read the invitation? It said to wear pink," one guest says.

"Who wears black to a King party? Rachel hates black!" says another.

You just want to run and hide. As you turn to leave, you spot your old friends – Flo, Fawn and Mary. You all used to be best friends. You called yourselves the Fair Four. Then they stopped calling you. They don't return your texts. You've heard they call themselves the Fair Three now.

You watch your old friends laughing by the punch bowl and realize how much you've missed them. You should go and say a quick hello. Then you look down at your dress. Maybe you should go home and change first.

TO JOIN THE FAIR THREE, TURN TO PAGE 65.

TO GO HOME, TURN TO PAGE 70.

"Yes, I'd be delighted!" you say.

Phil holds out his arm. You glide across the red carpet to the front of the hotel. Phil flashes his invitation at the bouncer, and the two of you step inside.

Phil leads you to the punch bowl and fills your glass. You clench it tightly, determined not to spill a drop on anyone this time.

"How do you know Rachel?" he asks you, sipping his punch.

"I've known her since she was a baby," you say vaguely. "How about you?"

"We go to the same school," Phil says. "Between you and me, I have a crush on her," he admits, blushing. "I was hoping to talk to her before she makes her grand entrance. I'm going to ask her for the first dance."

"That's a great idea, Phil. Do you know where she is now?" you ask him, trying not to sound too eager.

"I think she's taking a nap in her hotel room. It's up on the fourth floor," Phil says. "But I don't want to disturb her."

"Nonsense, this is the perfect time to talk to Rachel," you say. "I'll come with you."

This is perfect for you too. You'll follow Phil to Rachel's room and finally talk to the birthday girl. Just then you spot three women standing in the corner. You know them. It's Flo, Fawn and Mary. They used to be your best friends, before you stopped getting invited to parties. Maybe you should go and say hello. On the other hand, you told Phil you'd go and see Rachel.

TO TALK TO RACHEL WITH PHIL, TURN TO PAGE 63.

TO TALK TO FLO, FAWN AND MARY, TURN TO PAGE 65.

55

You shake your head. "No, thanks," you say. "I'm just passing by."

You walk quickly in the other direction while Phil stares at you. You turn the corner, and stop to think. That was close – you almost got caught. You need a better hiding place. You duck down an alley and head to the back of the hotel. As you get closer, you hear familiar voices through an open window. You lean in and listen.

"I don't know who she was," Phil says. "But she looked creepy. She was dressed all in black."

You peek through the window and see Phil talking to three women in the hotel reception. You recognize them – Flo, Fawn and Mary. They used to be your best friends a long time ago. But now they don't even return your texts.

"Maybe it was Millicent Fairy," says Fawn with a laugh.

"Wouldn't that be funny?" asks Mary.

"I can't *believe* we used to be friends with her," adds Flo.

You are seething with anger. They can't talk about you like that! Just as you are about to march through the back door and confront them, you hear another voice. You look up to see Rachel looking out over a balcony railing, talking on her mobile phone.

TO TRY TO GET RACHEL'S ATTENTION, TURN TO PAGE 58.

TO CONFRONT YOUR OLD FRIENDS, TURN TO PAGE 61.

You call to Rachel, but she doesn't hear you. Then you notice a large tree next to the hotel. You decide to climb it to get closer. Very carefully you climb onto one branch of the tree and then another. So far, so good. Just one more branch to go. You shimmy across a skinny branch that reaches over to Rachel's balcony.

"Rachel!" you call.

"Who's there?" Rachel says, putting her phone down and peering at the tree.

"I have a present for you," you say.

"Uh, OK. Who are you?" Rachel asks cautiously.

"I'm an old friend of your parents," you lie. "I knew you'd be busy during the party, so they told me I could give you my gift now."

Rachel nods and holds out her hand for the gift. You hold it out to her, but she can't reach it. You move further onto the branch.

CREAK! All of a sudden, the branch cracks under your weight. You cry out as it snaps and breaks. You flail in the air for a second. Then you fall hard onto the balcony . . . and onto Rachel. As you pick yourself up, you realize you've knocked the birthday girl out!

"Oh, no!" you cry. "People will never forgive me for this. I've got to get out of here."

You lean over the balcony, grab onto a branch and hoist yourself onto the tree. You climb down as fast as you can. As you reach the bottom, you adjust your dress. You stick your hand in your pockets. The fidget spinner! It's missing!

You look back up at the balcony and Rachel, who is still unconscious. Then you see it. The golden fidget spinner is resting beside her index finger.

Maybe there really is a curse, you think as you run away into the night.

THE END
TO FOLLOW ANOTHER PATH, TURN TO PAGE 7.

How dare they talk about you that way! You have had just about enough of your old friends talking behind your back. You march over to the back entrance of the hotel, ready to give them a piece of your mind. As you are about to walk inside, someone grabs you by the arm.

"Not so fast!" You turn around and see one of the bouncers from the front entrance. "Where's your invitation?"

"I lost it," you lie.

He shakes his head and steers you roughly off the premises. "Get out, and stay out!" he barks.

"Wait! I have my invitation right here!" you cry. You reach into your pocket. Something sharp stabs your finger. It's the spinning wheel fidget spinner.

TURN THE PAGE.

"Ouch!" you cry as you look at your
bloody finger.

You walk away feeling defeated and let out a
deep yawn. "I could try to sneak into the party
another way," you say to yourself. "But right now, I
just want to go home. I suddenly feel very sleepy."

THE END
TO FOLLOW ANOTHER PATH, TURN TO PAGE 7.

Phil follows you into the lift, and you both go up to the fourth floor. When you get to Rachel's room, you notice the door is ajar. You push open the door and find yourself in a grand hotel suite. On the bed lies Rachel, snoring.

"She's sleeping," you whisper to Phil.

His face falls in disappointment. "Let her sleep, I suppose," he says.

"No," you say. "You should wake her up. She can't be late to her own party!"

Phil steps nervously into the room and leans over the bed next to Rachel. You stand out of sight.

"Rachel," he says, gently shaking her shoulder.

Her eyes slowly open. "Phil? What are you doing here?"

"I've come to wake you," says Phil. "Your party is starting."

Rachel sits up and yawns. "I feel like I've been sleeping for a hundred years!" she says.

"Will you dance the first dance with me, Rachel?" Phil asks.

"Of course, Phil," says Rachel. "Let's go." Rachel hops down from the bed and rushes out of the room. Phil follows. He seems to have forgotten about you.

64 You touch the spinning wheel fidget spinner in your pocket as you stand in the lift. You never got a chance to explain yourself to Rachel or your friends. You can only hope you helped Rachel and Phil live happily ever after.

THE END
TO FOLLOW ANOTHER PATH, TURN TO PAGE 7.

You approach Flo, Fawn and Mary. Their eyes widen as they recognize you.

"Millicent!" gasps Fawn. "How dare you show your face here!"

Mary grabs Flo's arm. "We need to get Mr and Mrs King!"

"You threatened poor Rachel last time. Have you come to finish the job?" Fawn asks.

"I'm glad you brought that up," you say. But before you can finish, the lights dim and the crowd hushes. A spotlight shines on the entrance to the ballroom. Rachel appears, ready to make her grand entrance. She glides towards the centre of the room, waving to her guests. You wish you could be that graceful.

65

TURN THE PAGE.

You step closer to get a better view. Maybe you could even get a photo with the birthday girl! You reach into your pocket for your phone to take a quick selfie. As you pull out your phone, the spinning wheel fidget spinner falls from your pocket. It lands in front of Rachel.

"You dropped this," Rachel says, bending down to pick it up. As she does, she pricks her finger on the needle of the wheel.

"Ouch, you cut me!" Rachel cries. She looks at her bloody finger and starts to faint. Fawn and Mary rush to catch her before she falls.

"Really, Millicent! Will you stop at nothing to get attention?" Fawn hisses. Flo pushes past you. Your three old friends gather around Rachel and whisper. Then they whisk Rachel away.

You don't see Rachel again. You hear that she's staying at Mary's lake house in the woods for the rest of the summer. You hope that with Rachel away for a while, people will forget about what happened. But months go by, and you're still cut out of Castle City's social scene. You spend the rest of your days just as lonely as you were before.

THE END

TO FOLLOW ANOTHER PATH, TURN TO PAGE 7.

You walk into the reception and see two hotel staff getting into the lift. One has a pile of pink towels in her arms.

"I've got the special towels for the birthday girl," she says.

"Ugh. I know she's a King, but does she really need different towels?" asks the other.

They must be going to Rachel's room, you think.

You follow the houskeeping staff into the lift. One of them pushes the button for the fourth floor. You get an idea.

"There are the towels Rachel wanted," you say confidently. "I can take them to her. I'm her . . . godmother. Room 4–?"

"410," says the housekeeper, shoving the towels into your arms.

The lift door slides open, and you head down the corridor. Rachel's door is slightly ajar. Just as you are about to push the door open, a hand grabs your shoulder. You whirl around.

"What are you doing?" says a handsome young man. He eyes your dress. "You don't look like a housekeeper."

"Just doing a favour," you say. "I was on my way up here anyway to visit Rachel. I'm a friend of her parents. We hang out all the time."

"I'm Phil, Rachel's boyfriend," he snaps. "And I've never seen you with Rachel's parents before."

69

Boyfriend? You could explain everything to Phil and ask him to talk to Rachel. But he seems suspicious. You might be better off getting rid of Phil and talking to Rachel alone.

TO TALK TO PHIL, TURN TO PAGE 73.

TO GO INTO RACHEL'S ROOM ALONE, TURN TO PAGE 75.

Coming here was a mistake. You wanted to fit in with these people so badly, but all they do is laugh at you. You turn and run out of the ballroom as fast as you can. Behind you, you hear the entire party bursting into laughter.

"Poor Millicent. She'll never be like us," you hear Mary say.

"She wore black! Can you believe it?" Fawn cackles.

"Why did she even bother coming?" asks Flo.

You burst out of the back door and into the dark garden. You're crying so hard that you can't see where you're going. And that's when you fall. Hard. You land flat on your face.

As you lie on the ground, you hear a sweet voice above you. "Are you OK?"

You look up to see Rachel standing over you, wearing a shimmering pink dress.

"Yeah, I'm just great," you sob. "I made an absolute fool of myself at that party!" You slowly sit up. "I used to be one of them a long time ago," you say, pointing to the crowd inside. "But once again, I've ended up all alone. I'll never get those people to accept me. All because of a silly spinning wheel!"

"A spinning wheel?" says Rachel. "Are you Millicent Fairy?"

"Yes!" you wail.

"I've heard about you," Rachel says. "You are hilarious! Cinderella still talks about her punch-soaked dress. I think people in this town need to get a sense of humour." Rachel grabs both your hands. "Here, let's get you up."

Rachel pulls you to your feet. "You're going back to this party . . . as my guest."

You wipe your eyes and follow Rachel inside. You spend the rest of the party dancing with Rachel and her friends. All night, the Fair Three glare at you from across the room.

THE END

TO FOLLOW ANOTHER PATH, TURN TO PAGE 7.

"Let me explain," you begin. "I—"

"Quiet!" Phil says sharply. "Who invited you to this party, anyway? And what are you wearing? The invitation said to wear pink."

You are about to get caught, so you decide to lie. "Don't tell me to be quiet," you snap. "Rachel isn't even in there. Come with me. I know where she is."

Phil frowns, but he follows you anyway. As you and Phil get into the lift, you discreetly text your limo driver. Your limo pulls up just as you and Phil leave the hotel.

"She's in my limo," you tell Phil. "See? She's right there," you say, pointing into the dark window.

"Why would she be in your limo?" Phil asks suspiciously.

"Like I said, I'm a friend of her parents," you say quickly. "If you don't believe me, look for yourself."

Phil opens the limo door and looks inside. Suddenly, you shove him in. Then you hop in and lock the doors.

Phil tries to open the door. "Hey! Let me out!" he yells.

You tell your driver to go – fast! As the limo zips through the city, you try to tell your story to Phil, but he won't listen. He just yells and bangs on the window. You get tired of all the noise he's making, so you pop a sleeping pill or two into his yelling mouth. He drops off to sleep. When you get to your house, you and your limo driver carry Phil up to the attic. You decide not to let him out until he listens to you, even if it takes a hundred years.

THE END
TO FOLLOW ANOTHER PATH, TURN TO PAGE 7.

You throw the towels at Phil's head. "Hey!" he yells, stumbling backwards.

You run into Rachel's room and slam the door shut. It locks automatically behind you. Rachel wakes up with a start.

"Who are you?" Rachel gasps. "What are you doing in my room?"

"My name is Millicent, and I just want to give you a birthday gift," you say. You hold out the spinning wheel fidget spinner. You expect to see Rachel's eyes light up, but she just stares at you and the gift, horrified.

75

"Millicent? Do you mean Millicent Fairy?" she asks.

TURN THE PAGE.

"Yes, I'm Millicent, but . . . ," you say.

"My parents told me about you. They said you tried to hurt me as a baby," Rachel yells. "Stay away from me, you evil witch. Security!"

Two security guards unlock the door and rush into the room, followed by an angry Phil and Mr and Mrs King. The guards grab your arms, and the spinning wheel falls to the floor.

"Please, just let me explain!" you say, as Mrs King puts her arms around a trembling Rachel.

"It's Millicent," Rachel says, pointing at you.

"She sneaked in while I was sleeping. Who knows what she planned to do with that fidget spinner! There's a sharp needle on it. See?"

Mr King looks at your gift with disgust. He picks it up and turns to you. "I've called the police. I hope you like prison food, you lunatic," he says.

The police arrive, and you are arrested. You are charged with trespassing, stalking and attempted assault with a fidget spinner. Eventually, the case goes to trial. Everyone in Castle City turns up to watch the trial. Rachel, Phil and the Kings testify against you. You don't stand a chance. You are sentenced to prison, far from Castle City. You won't go to another party again.

THE END
TO FOLLOW ANOTHER PATH, TURN TO PAGE 7.

CHAPTER 4

The sleeping Martian

Thousands of years ago forest fires, earthquakes and floods destroyed much of Earth. Wars destroyed the rest of it. Humans could no longer live on the planet. There was no food, clean air or water. Luckily scientists built a community on the planet Mars. Humans have lived on Mars ever since.

For a while Mars was a peaceful and orderly place, governed by the gentle President King. Your father was a top official in King's government. You spent your childhood in Capital City playing with your best friend Prince, President King's son.

But it turned out that humans weren't the only life-forms in outer space. Several years ago, the evil fairy – ruler of the planet Mal – attacked Mars and its people. She and her alien minions invaded Capital City, killed President King and kidnapped Prince. The evil fairy returned to planet Mal and now rules Mars from afar.

After the attack, those who did not give their allegiance to the evil fairy were forced to flee Capital City. They scattered to the far-off regions of Mars, hiding in caves and craters. You and your father managed to escape too. Since then, humans have had to move from cave to cave to avoid the evil fairy's detection.

Many have tried to defeat the evil fairy and rescue Prince, but none have succeeded. You've spent your childhood training to be a warrior. You are determined to find your friend.

Your father taught you how to use a laser gun, fight in combat and fly a spacecraft. He has always believed that you would be the one to defeat the evil fairy and bring peace back to Mars.

After years of training, you are ready. You put on your spacesuit and find your father. When you tell him you're ready to save Prince, he nods. "The people of Mars are relying on you, Briar," your father says. "I know you will succeed."

You grab your laser gun and slide into your tiny spacecraft. Then you set planet Mal as your destination and zoom off. Mars soon becomes a speck behind you.

TURN THE PAGE.

Up ahead you see the twinkling lights of three spaceships. They seem to be heading straight for you. There aren't many friendly travellers in outer space. You wonder if you should fire at the spaceships. Or you could try to lose them.

TO SHOOT AT THE SPACESHIPS, TURN TO PAGE 83.

TO ZOOM AWAY, TURN TO PAGE 84.

You whirl your spacecraft around, aiming your space guns at the approaching spaceships. Their lights grow brighter and brighter, nearly blinding you. You fire into the brightness, but your space guns sound like toys in the roar of the ships surrounding you.

Your radio beeps – short, short … long … long. You recognize the secret code of the Pixies, three aliens who helped the humans battle the evil fairy and her minions during the invasion.

You decipher their code. The message says: WE ARE THE PIXIES. WE HAVE RECEIVED WORD THAT PRINCE MAY STILL BE ON MARS. WE CAN HELP IF YOU COME WITH US.

TO CONTINUE TO PLANET MAL, TURN TO PAGE 85.

TO GO WITH THE PIXIES BACK TO MARS, TURN TO PAGE 87.

You hit the throttle and zoom ahead. You manage to lose the twinkling spaceships.

When you get close to Mal, you scope out the planet. To your right, a dark fortress glows. This must be the evil fairy's fortress. To your left, a dark tower reaches into the sky.

You start to head towards the fortress when you hear crackling on your radio. You turn the radio dial until you can hear a few words.

"... Prince ..." a male voice says. "... tower ..."

The voice doesn't sound familiar, but it could be Prince. After all, you were only a child the last time you spoke to him. Perhaps you should explore the tower. But the message could be a trap for nosy humans venturing too close to Mal.

84

TO INVESTIGATE THE TOWER, TURN TO PAGE 89.

TO GO TO THE FORTRESS, TURN TO PAGE 97.

You've searched every cave and crater on Mars looking for Prince. He has to be on Mal.

"I will continue on to planet Mal," you radio.

The Pixies radio back. Their message says: VERY WELL. BUT PLEASE ACCEPT OUR GIFTS. SAFE JOURNEY.

Gifts? you wonder. Just then, something slams against your ship's hull. The craft shakes, and you are jostled around inside.

OOPS! the message says. JUST A MINOR SCRATCH.

You pull the cargo into your spacecraft and zoom off. As you get near planet Mal, you inspect the gifts. One is a long sword. You recognize it as the Blue Sword. It is so strong, it can spear the evil fairy's space dragons. The other gift is the Red Shield. It can protect you against fireballs.

You fly the rest of the way to planet Mal. Up ahead, you spot the evil fairy's fortress. Suddenly you notice something large flying towards you. You steer your ship behind a huge boulder so you are not seen. Then you see it – a giant space dragon! The evil fairy is riding on its back.

You think about all the people who have died fighting against the evil fairy. Anger boils up in your chest. You want to charge the dragon and kill the evil fairy once and for all. But you aren't sure you can defeat a dragon head-on. Perhaps you should come up with a solid plan first.

86

TO CHARGE THE DRAGON, TURN TO PAGE 91.

TO FLY AWAY, TURN TO PAGE 94.

Although you want to defeat the evil fairy, saving Prince is your priority. And the Pixies seem to have good intel.

SHOW ME THE WAY, you radio back.

The three Pixie spaceships hover around you. One ship is blue, one is red and the other is green. The Pixies instruct you to fly your ship into the green spaceship's loading dock and travel along with her. You do as they say. You leave your ship and climb into the green spaceship's control room. A Pixie in a green spacesuit sits at the controls. You look around. Everything is green – the walls, the ceiling and all the controls.

"My name is Green," says the Pixie.

"I never would have guessed!" you laugh.

"We've determined that Prince is on Mars," Green tells you. "We'll check Capital City first. We can enter the city through the underground caves that surround it."

Just then, you spot a tower you've never seen before on Mars. It looks like the towers you've heard about on planet Mal. Perhaps the evil fairy has Prince trapped inside.

You turn to Green. "We should explore that tower," you say, pointing below.

"Our intel says to go to Capital City," says Green. "If you want to go to the tower, you must go alone."

TO GET IN YOUR SHIP AND GO TO THE TOWER, TURN TO PAGE 89.

TO GO WITH THE PIXIES TO THE CAVES, TURN TO PAGE 99.

88

You take off towards the tower in your spaceship. As you get closer, you see a weak green light glowing in one of the windows of the tower. *Could that be where Prince is?* you wonder.

You start to descend to the ground. Suddenly you see inky, black shapes surrounding the tower. Alien minions! Millions of them! There's no way you can land among them to get into the tower.

Just as you are about to give up and zoom away, you notice that the tower has a flat roof. Perfect! You could land your ship there, and climb down the thick, thorny barbed wire that surrounds the tower. Then you could enter through one of the tower's windows.

TURN THE PAGE.

But as you lower the landing gear, you notice that the roof is covered in thorny barbed wire as well. The wire wraps around your spacecraft.

"Come on!" you yell as you shift gears. You can't move forwards or backwards. You're stuck! You can't open the spacecraft's door either.

The minions have noticed you on the roof. They climb the walls of the tower and head towards your ship. Slowly they start taking apart your ship, piece by piece. They will be inside in seconds. You grab your laser gun, ready to fight them off. But you know there are too many to fight. You are doomed to join the other lost warriors who tried to rescue Prince.

THE END
TO FOLLOW ANOTHER PATH, TURN TO PAGE 7.

The anger inside you builds. In a fit of rage, you decide to attack the dragon. You put the controls on autopilot. Then you hop out of the spacecraft with your sword and shield.

"Here we go," you say. You cling to the front of the spacecraft and charge full speed at the dragon.

The dragon sees your attack and opens its mouth, showing its giant teeth. Suddenly a fireball comes out of its throat, then another. The fireballs bounce off your shield, but your face still feels like it's melting. As the dragon opens its mouth to launch another fireball at you, you leap from the top of the spaceship, brandishing your sword.

91

TURN THE PAGE.

You jump onto the dragon and plunge the
sword deep into its neck. It bucks and kicks.

"Noooo!" the evil fairy cries.

Both of you are thrown from the dragon. You
roll to your feet, ready for battle. The dragon is
dead, but the evil fairy is nowhere to be seen. You
look around. She has disappeared.

You get back into your spaceship and fly home. As you come closer to Mars, your communications radio buzzes. You dial in.

"Hello?" says a voice at the other end. "Is anyone out there?"

"Yes, this is Briar from the planet Mars. Who am I speaking to?" you ask.

"Briar? Is that you?" says the voice. "This is Prince! The Pixies rescued me. They told me you were searching for me."

You can't believe you are talking to Prince. Tears well in your eyes. When you return to Mars, a party 93 is thrown for you, Prince and the Pixies. The fight is far from over, though. The evil fairy is still out there. But with Prince's help, you can make Mars a place where everyone can live happily ever after.

THE END

TO FOLLOW ANOTHER PATH, TURN TO PAGE 7.

You zoom away from the space dragon. You'll have to think of another way to destroy the evil fairy and rescue Prince.

As you are plotting your next move, you see something looming behind you. Hundreds of little black spaceships rise from the surface of planet Mal. Inside the ships, you see the glowing green faces of the alien minions.

You point your spaceship's guns at the minion ships and fire. Your guns destroy some of them, but the minions keep coming. Their ships swirl around you. You try to zoom away, but a minion spaceship launches a net. It snares your spacecraft and drags it back down to planet Mal.

Your ship slams onto the surface of planet Mal. You're a little shaken, but you're OK. You look out of the window and see that the minions have landed. They are heading towards your spaceship. Then you hear it – the evil fairy's laughter. She's here too.

She's not getting away this time, you think. You quickly grab the sword and shield the Pixies gave

you and jump out of your spaceship.

As soon as your feet touch the ground, the aliens attack. You swing your sword. Suddenly rays of green, red and blue shoot out of the sword, zapping the minions. They fall to the ground one by one.

Then you turn to the evil fairy. She picks up her magic staff and crashes it onto the ground. The remaining minions scatter. Then she takes aim. A ball of purple light comes out of the staff, straight at you. You raise your shield. The purple fireball bounces off and arcs back towards the evil fairy.

"Ahhh!" she cries, as the fireball hits her. She is reduced to a pile of ashes. Without their leader, the minions slink away. You look around. The evil fairy and her alien minions have been defeated. The people of Mars are safe once again.

You get back into your ship and speed away from planet Mal. There is only one thing left to do.

"Now to find Prince," you say to yourself.

THE END
TO FOLLOW ANOTHER PATH, TURN TO PAGE 7.

You zoom towards the evil fairy's fortress. It's large and dark – and surprisingly quiet. No guards stand at the doors, and you can't see any evil minions.

You land and get out of your spaceship. As you approach the huge fortress, you hear a voice behind you.

"Looking for me?" the evil fairy asks.

You whirl to face her. She is larger than you'd expected. Her alien face glows green, and her long cloak shimmers black and purple.

"You are about to be defeated, evil fairy!" you cry. You point your laser gun at her and shoot, but she doesn't fall. The lasers bounce off her.

"Nice try, human!" the evil fairy says. She points her magic staff and fires. The force launches you into the air, and you land hard on the ground.

The evil fairy cackles as she approaches you.
You try to scramble away, but she pins you down
with her staff. In her other hand, she holds a
circular weapon. A needle launches from the
weapon and stabs your finger.

"Ready to join your friend Prince?" she asks
as your eyes close. You fall unconscious. The evil
fairy's minions carry you to a cave and lay you
next to Prince, where you will both sleep forever.

THE END
TO FOLLOW ANOTHER PATH, TURN TO PAGE 7.

The three spaceships touch down just outside Capital City. You and Green hop out from her spaceship and greet the others – Red and Blue. You look around. Several caves and craters surround the city.

"Which one leads into Capital City?" you ask.

"They all do," Blue says. "We just have to choose one."

You step into one of the dark caves with Red, Blue and Green following behind you. You shine a light into the depths of the cave. You're sure you see something move. You sweep your torch around the cave, but nothing is there.

"Let's keep going," you say. You and the Pixies move deeper into the cave. Suddenly slinky, inky black creatures dart out from the walls and race towards you. Their eyes glow greenish-yellow.

"Minions!" yells Green.

"It's a trap!" cries Blue.

"Attack!" you yell, pulling out your laser gun. This is the moment you've been training for. You point your laser and pull the trigger, but nothing happens. It's jammed!

"Don't just stand there," Red cries. "Do something!"

TO ATTACK THE MINIONS, TURN TO PAGE 101.

TO RUN, TURN TO PAGE 103.

You've waited all this time to battle the evil minions and rescue Prince. You are not running away now. There has to be a way. You hold your laser gun with both hands and swing at the minions. They go flying like tennis balls. Behind you, the Pixies are slashing at the minions with their swords. But the minions keep coming. You know you can only fend them off for so long.

As you swing at another minion, you feel something pop in your gun. The force of the blow has un-jammed the gun.

"Come on!" you yell to the Pixies as you run through the cave, blasting the minions away.

At last, you emerge from the cave. You and the Pixies roll boulders over the cave's mouth to seal the minions inside.

You and the Pixies make your way through Capital City. It lies in ruins. The only building still standing is the president's mansion.

"That could be the building that Prince is in," you say. You head towards the president's mansion. Inside, you race up the stairs towards what was once Prince's room. You burst through the door, and there he is, lying fast asleep on the bed.

"Go on, then," says Red behind you. "Kiss him."

"Kiss him?" you ask in shock.

"The cells on your lips will act as an antidote to the sleeping poison," said Red.

"But not until—" Green says.

"I can hear something. Perhaps the minions have found us!" interrupts Blue.

TO KISS PRINCE, TURN TO PAGE 104.

TO FIND OUT WHAT THE NOISE IS, TURN TO PAGE 105.

You know you can't defeat the minions without a gun. They'll just kill you, and you'll be no help to Prince if you're dead.

You and the Pixies scramble out of the cave. The minions are close at your heels. You sprint towards the Pixies' spaceships.

"Quick! Get into the closest one!" yells Blue.

You and the three Pixies tumble into a purple spaceship. Your chest heaves.

"Phew, that was close!" you gasp.

"Welcome aboard," a voice says. You turn to see the evil fairy sitting in the pilot's seat. Her green lips break into a grin. Then the ship soars into the air. "Let's go on a little journey," she says. "To planet Mal!"

103

THE END
TO FOLLOW ANOTHER PATH, TURN TO PAGE 7.

You lean down and give Prince a peck on the lips. He slowly opens his eyes. "Briar? Is that you?" he asks.

You are about to answer when suddenly you feel faint. Your eyes are so heavy, you can't keep them open.

"I was going to say, kiss him after you put on this protective lip balm," Green says holding a small vial. "That would have protected you from the sleeping poison."

You drift off to sleep as you hear Blue's words.

"Thanks a lot, Red," Blue says. "Now we have another sleeping beauty on our hands."

THE END
TO FOLLOW ANOTHER PATH, TURN TO PAGE 7.

You turn towards the door with your laser gun, ready to battle the minions. But the corridor is empty.

"It's nothing," you say. "The minions are still trapped."

"Now kiss him, Briar," Red says.

"But put this protective balm on your lips first," instructs Green, handing you a small vial. "It will protect you from the sleeping poison the evil fairy covered him in."

You apply the balm to your lips. Then you bend over and lean towards Prince. Suddenly Prince's eyes start to open.

105

"Briar? Is that you?" Prince says, jolting awake. "What are you doing? Where am I?"

Blue sighs. "You see, Red? Waking someone up with a kiss is just a silly fairy tale after all!"

THE END

TO FOLLOW ANOTHER PATH, TURN TO PAGE 7.

CHAPTER 5

Sleeping Beauty through the ages

The classic tale of *Sleeping Beauty* has a beautiful princess, a sleeping spell and a handsome prince who can break the spell. But the story we know today has various origins that go back hundreds of years.

One of the first stories of a sleeping beauty is *Perceforest*. It was printed in 1528. In *Perceforest*, a knight called Troylus hears that his love Zellandine has fallen asleep and will not wake up. He rushes to her side but is unable to wake her. Eventually Zellandine gives birth to their child.

The baby sucks on her finger and draws out the poison. Zellandine finally wakes up.

In 1697 Charles Perrault wrote *The Sleeping Beauty in the Wood*. In this story, seven fairies are invited to a party for the newborn princess. An eighth fairy, angry at not being invited, curses the baby. The curse says that one day she will prick her finger on a spinning wheel and die. Another fairy changes the curse, so the princess will not die. Instead, she will sleep for one hundred years. The king orders all spinning wheels to be burned. When the princess is a teenager, she comes across a spinning wheel, pricks her finger and falls asleep. The good fairy puts the entire castle to sleep as well. One hundred years later, a prince comes upon the castle. The sleeping beauty wakes up when he kneels at her bedside. The two eventually marry and have two children. The prince's mother, who is an ogre, tries to eat the two children. But the children are saved by the royal cook.

Brothers Jacob and Wilhelm Grimm retold Perrault's tale with their story, *Little Briar-Rose*, in 1812. The Grimm's version is similar to Perrault's, but it has thirteen fairies instead of eight. The Grimms also added the famous kiss that wakes up the sleeping princess. They left out the ogre from the previous story.

In 1959 Walt Disney produced an animated film called *Sleeping Beauty*. In the film there are only three good fairies – Flora, Fauna and Merryweather. The evil fairy is called Maleficent. In the film, Prince Phillip uses a magical sword and shield to battle Maleficent, who has turned into a dragon.

One of the most recent films about Sleeping Beauty is *Maleficent*, which was released in 2014. This film tells the untold story of Maleficent, who comes to regret her curse on Aurora, the sleeping beauty.

OTHER PATHS TO EXPLORE

1. Imagine your own *Sleeping Beauty* fairy tale. Where does the story take place? How is it different from the original tale? How does the story end?

2. Chapter 3 tells the *Sleeping Beauty* story from the villain's point of view. After reading this story, do you think Millicent was good or evil? Why or why not?

3. In Chapter 5 we learn about the different versions of the *Sleeping Beauty* tale. How are these versions different? How are they similar?

FIND OUT MORE

BOOKS

A Treasury of Fairy Tales and Myths, Mary Hoffman (DK Children, 2018)

Sleeping Beauty, Magic Master: A Graphic Novel (Far out Fairy Tales), Stephanie True Peters (Raintree, 2016)

Usborne Illustrated Fairy Tales (Anthologies and Treasuries), Rosie Dickins (Usborne, 2007)

WEBSITES

www.bbc.co.uk/guides/zy2m3k7
Get some useful tips on how to write your own fairy tale!

www.bbc.co.uk/learning/schoolradio/subjects/ english/hans_christian_andersen
Listen to some classic fairy tales by Hans Christian Andersen.

LOOK FOR OTHER BOOKS IN THIS SERIES: